For Leo

First published in Great Britain in 2017 by Simon and Schuster UK Ltd
1st Floor, 222 Gray's Inn Road, London, WC1X 8HB • A CBS Company • Text
and illustrations copyright © 2017 Nicola Slater • The right of Nicola Slater to
be identified as the author and illustrator of this work has been asserted by her
in accordance with the Copyright, Designs and Patents Act, 1988 • All rights
reserved, including the right of reproduction in whole or in part in any form
A CIP catalogue record for this book is available from the British Library upon
request 978-1-4711-6305-0 (HB) • 978-1-4711-4621-3 (PB) • Printed in China
10 9 8 7 6 5 4 3 2 1

SIMON & SCHUSTER

London   New York   Sydney   Toronto   New Delhi

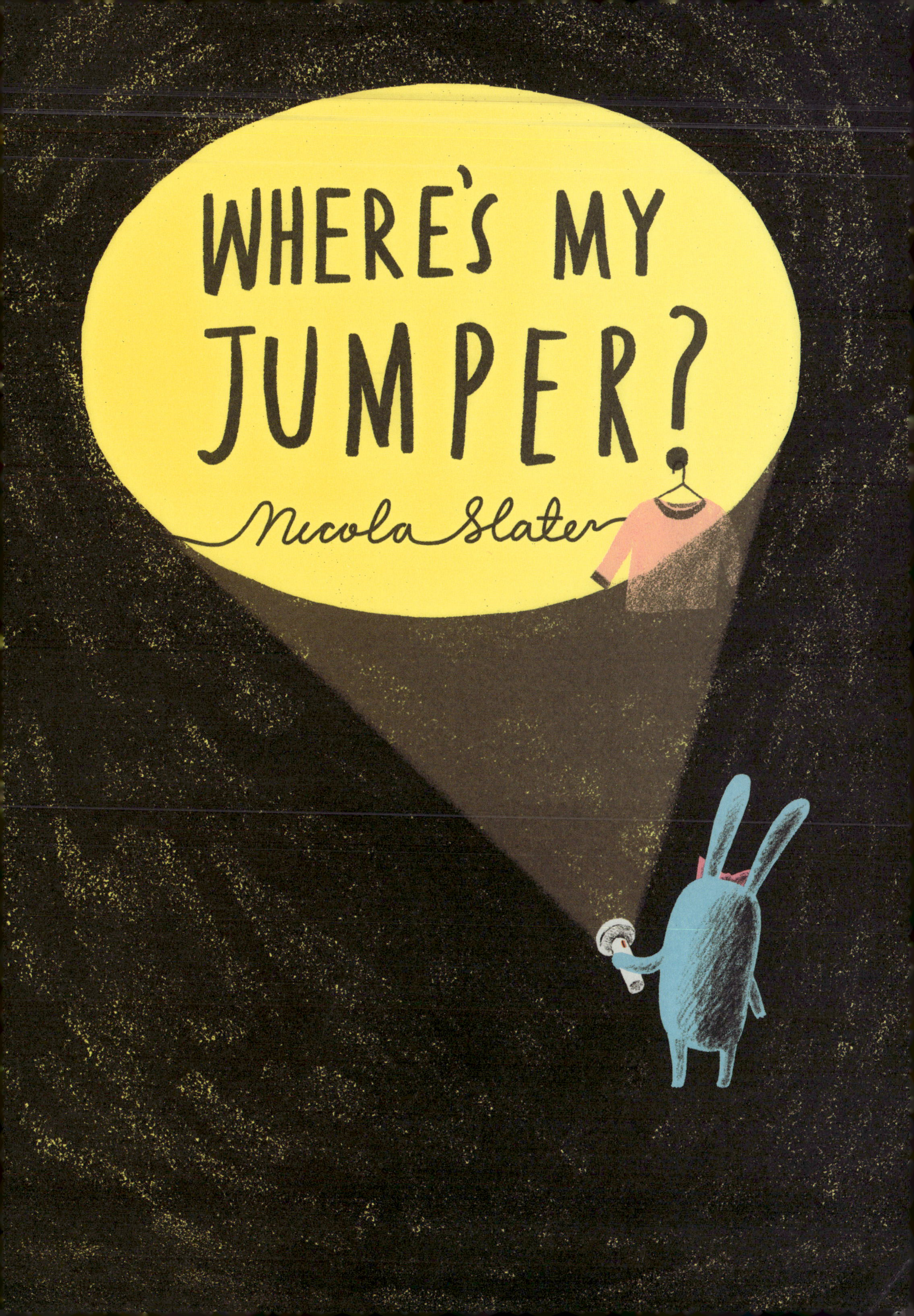
WHERE'S MY JUMPER?
Nicola Slater

Rudy LOVED his pink jumper.

It was a little bit short and showed his tummy. But it was his favourite.

Then one Monday he woke up and . . .

. . . it had **gone!**

WHERE'S MY JUMPER?

The **TEN** tumbling cats hanging out in his wardrobe hadn't seen a thing.

So Rudy ran downstairs.

The **NINE** jiving llamas in fancy-pants pyjamas didn't even know he was there.

But the **EIGHT** prima pigerinas pirouetting in the kitchen were delighted Rudy had stopped by for tea.

Then he heard the cellar door creak . . .

He slipped past the **SEVEN** ski-dogs
slaloming on the stairs.
Plenty of pink knitwear here. But no jumper.

He headed back upstairs.

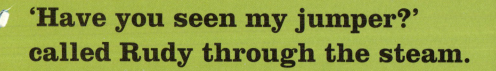

'Have you seen my jumper?'
called Rudy through the steam.

Follow the trail
follow the string
to find your favourite
woolly thing!

**trilled SIX soapy blackbirds
in the shower.**

So Rudy did.

Out of the window and into the pool with **FIVE** jibber-jabbering sea creatures.

Unfortunately Rudy didn't speak Octopus.

So off he went . . .

Could his jumper really
be here?
'Don't be silly!'
'Don't be daft!'
'Don't get lost!'
'Go back!'
said FOUR muttering mice.

Rudy clambered his way up and found **TWO** queuing crocs.

Rudy was sad.
Even **TWO** passing foxes had
their super-special jumpers on!

His jumper was gone,

lost,

vanished!

Rudy wondered who might want his jumper.

Who was the cheekiest person he knew?

Could it be...

. . . Trudy? **YES!**

His number **ONE** sister.

Rudy loved his jumper,
but he loved Trudy more.

Perhaps it was time
for a new one after all!